When Mules Flew on

Magnolia Street

When Mules Flew on
Magnolia Street

Angela Johnson
illustrated by John Ward

Alfred A. Knopf　　**New York**

To Alyssa and DJ

THIS IS A BORZOI BOOK PUBLISHED BY ALFRED A. KNOPF

Text copyright © 2000 by Angela Johnson
Illustrations copyright © 2000 by John Ward
All rights reserved under International and Pan-American Copyright Conventions.
Published in the United States of America by Alfred A. Knopf, a division of Random
House, Inc., New York, and simultaneously in Canada by Random House of Canada
Limited, Toronto. Distributed by Random House, Inc., New York.

www.randomhouse.com/kids

Library of Congress Cataloging-in-Publication Data

Johnson, Angela.
When mules flew on Magnolia Street / by Angela Johnson ; illustrated by John Ward.
p.   cm.
Summary: In the summertime Charlie goes fishing with her friends, investigates the
mysterious disappearance of the entire Carter family, meets new neighbors, and finds that
she and her older brother can be friends.
ISBN 0-679-89077-7 (trade) — ISBN 0-679-99077-1 (lib. bdg.)
[1. Friendship—Fiction. 2. Afro-Americans—Fiction.] I. Ward, John, 1963– ill. II. Title.
PZ7.J629 Wm   2000   [Fic]—dc21   00-035742

KNOPF, BORZOI BOOKS, and the colophon are registered
trademarks of Random House, Inc.

First Edition

Printed in the United States of America
December 2000
10 9 8 7 6 5 4 3 2 1

CONTENTS

CHAPTER ONE

We Go Fishing

School is out for summer! So today is the first summer-vacation fishing trip for me and my two best friends, Lump and Billy. And here is what I'm taking:

3 baloney sandwiches

12 comic books

3 Big Swooshie Fruit Punch Drink boxes

1 net

1 pound of cheese (the fish love it)

1 can of mosquito repellent

1 fishing pole

1 pail with ice (and it's a good thing Mom's dropping us off, 'cause that pail of ice would be heavy to carry all the way to the river at the end of Magnolia Street)

1 Goober Kids book (I'll share)

I don't think it's too much to take with me, even though Mom said something about how huge my backpack is. We love to fish, even though we're not very good at it.

The fish like us 'cause they love the cheese we put on our hooks.

I could fish all day long. My big brother, Sid, says he doesn't know why we don't just throw the cheese in the water with bread so the fish can make themselves sandwiches. He says we're feeding them, not fishing for them....

The sun came up a few minutes ago, and I'm done packing. Mom wasn't looking too good, though. She was all huddled over her cup of coffee and she wasn't smiling like she usually does in the morning.

I looked at her feet.

"Mom, are you going to drive us fishing in your bunny slippers?"

She looked down and stared at her slippers

like she didn't know how the bunnies got on her feet. The bunnies were a birthday gift from me to her. Mom always wears them. She says they're better than pets because they don't shed fur on the sofa and they don't eat out of the garbage can.

My mom is a little different from most people. I like her a lot.

"Well, I think the girls won't mind driving you and the boys to the fishing hole. They've combed their ears and brushed their noses."

"Huh?" I said.

"The bunnies are going. Do you think Lump and Billy will like them?"

"Lump and Billy won't mind. Billy's mom wears a hat with a propeller, and Lump's uncle always wears yellow Hawaiian shirts."

"Wow," Mom said.

"Yeah, they all dress pretty cool."

"Well, I'm glad you think the bunny girls are cool clothing."

"Hey, I wouldn't have gotten them for you otherwise."

Just as Mom went to look for her car keys, Lump and Billy fell into the kitchen.

Lump asked, "Are you ready to go fishing?"

"We're ready and waiting," Billy called out to anybody in the room who might have been listening.

We sang a fishing song till Mom dropped us off on the side of the road and waved good-bye.

A-fishin' we will go.
A-fishin' we will go.
Put down your plate and eat some bait.
A-fishin' we will go.

We make up songs whenever we go fishing, and never afterward remember anything we've sung. We've made up thousands of fishing songs. I think the fish like them, too, even though everyone says the noise scares them.

Me, Lump, and Billy grabbed all our fishing gear and ran down the ravine to the river.

It was a beautiful morning.

We walked for a few minutes along the river. Water bugs danced on the surface, and we listened to katydids calling. We have a special place that's just big enough for us. The bank is sandy, and there's enough room to put all our gear down and still stretch out while we're fishing.

"Great!" Lump said as he started to bait the fishhooks with cheese.

"Nothing like fishing," Billy said as he pulled out a few comic books and the mosquito spray.

I took the Big Swooshies and put them into the river so the water would keep them cool.

It's early in the summer, and the water was still cold. The sun hadn't warmed up our part of the river yet.

I also tied up some loose ends of the net. It got a little torn last time, when Billy got bored with fishing and went looking for elk upriver. Even though Lump said he didn't think elk lived this far south, it didn't stop Billy, who ripped the net catching what he first thought was a bear but which turned out to be an old barbecue.

When Billy gets something in his head, you better not get in his way. It's best to join in; mostly, we do.

Soon we were all waiting for the fish to come. This is always my favorite part of fishing— waiting and looking into the water. It's exciting thinking that a fish could bite at any moment.

Mostly, though, they just take the bait, not the hook. Then we feed them more.

"It's good to be out of school for the summer," Lump said.

"Yeah," I said. "I think the teachers needed a break. They were starting to daydream and not pay attention to their work."

Billy said, "I caught Ms. Thorton playing with a yo-yo before class a couple of days before summer vacation."

Lump said, "The whole class caught Mr. Kane blowing bubbles at his desk the day school let out."

"I feel sorry for the teachers. It's hard for them all year long. I hope a few of them are out fishing someplace."

"Yeah," said Lump.

"Yeah," said Billy.

I threw a couple of chunks of cheese into the water for the fish who might not make it to the fishing poles. Sid might be right about them making sandwiches, but I wouldn't tell him that.

It got very quiet on the river. We got quiet, too. Nothing like fishing, with the sun high in the sky.

Lump took out the sandwiches. We all love baloney. It's another one of the good parts of fishing. I took the Big Swooshies out of the river, and we drank them like we'd been in the desert all day. You'd just dry up and get blown away like a leaf if it wasn't for Big Swooshies. Fishing is hard, fun, and long....

After the sandwiches and the Swooshies, we must have fallen asleep, 'cause when we woke up, the sun had warmed up the riverbank and our fishing poles were gone!

We all woke up at the same time. Maybe there was a noise in the woods surrounding us. Maybe someone blew a horn on Magnolia Street. Or maybe three fish took the bait at the same time, pulling our fishing poles away from the riverbank and waking us up because they were laughing so hard that we could hear it coming from underwater.

Billy thought it was the last one.

Lump thought it was probably all of them.

I thought we'd just slept so hard for so long, like big old warthogs, it was just a matter of time before we woke up.

"What are we going to do?" Billy said as we watched our poles float gently in the middle of the river.

"Only one thing we *can* do," I said.

Lump blew a bubble and nodded and said, "Yep, only one thing."

Well, it was a good thing it had warmed up. It was also a good thing we were all excellent swimmers (even though the river comes up only to our waists), 'cause we were in the middle of the river for a long time.

I found river weed while I was trying to untangle the fishing lines. Lump decided Billy

would look good with it on top of his head. I thought Lump would, too.

In the end they both looked completely hysterical—like swamp monsters!

Billy splashed and jumped in and out of the water while I tried some river weed on myself.

Lump squished in his wet clothes as he went along the bank collecting frogs in the net. He got about twenty of them. They croaked loudly into the warm afternoon air.

After we sat in the water awhile listening to their song, we took handfuls of them at a time and let them go back to what they were doing. Then we screamed and splashed each other till we probably scared off the rest of the fish.

We laughed till we couldn't stand it anymore. After a while we waded back to the riverbank. Our wet clothes felt heavy as blankets. Lump passed the comic books around, and if somebody had come by us in a boat, they would have wondered where the vine-covered sea monsters reading comics had come from.

A little while later we threw the rest of the cheese to the fish and drank the last of our Big Swooshies. Then each of us read a chapter of the Goober Kids out loud.

The five o'clock whistle at the peanut butter factory had blown when I heard Mom calling from the top of the ravine. We packed everything in a hurry and ran up to the street. After we'd loaded the car with everything but fish, we rolled down the car window and sang more fishing songs. Real loud.

It's really true, I thought as we headed toward home, Lump and Billy and me screaming our songs, there really is nothing like fishing!

CHAPTER TWO

A Mystery

(Where're the Carters?)

Something weird is happening on Magnolia Street. I thought I knew what it was all about, but it turned out to be something totally different. At first I was kind of scared.

I even told Sid all about it, so I know I was pretty worried.

It didn't start off like a mystery. At least not like the mysteries in books I read. Usually, in those books, somebody is running down a dark road in the rain or has moved into an old house that has a secret room he can't get into.

This mystery is the Carter family. They disappeared.

A huge family, with about ten kids, five dogs (one that barked at everybody), three cats, and six guinea pigs, one day just wasn't there at all. I mean, just like that!

One minute Ben Carter was squirting water at everyone with his mom's hose, and his little sister Dana was selling lemonade at a stand while their sister Vicky slept in the hammock in the front yard (though how she can sleep with all those people around I do not know). The next minute they were all gone.

Well, not exactly a minute. It was two days.

I went to borrow a few crab apples off their tree when I noticed that there weren't even lawn chairs in the front yard anymore. All the Big Wheels, bikes, and wading pools had also disappeared.

Usually you could hear laughing and yelling real early in the morning at the Carters'. This morning no dog barked, and there wasn't one sound from the house.

I went closer and I noticed that the bamboo shades on the front door were gone. The wind chimes that made tinkling sounds were gone, too.

So I climbed onto the porch and looked in. I guess I half expected to see most everybody in time-out, the house being so quiet and everything.

I ran the half a block to my house, crashing into my mom just as she was getting into her car to go to work. She'd dumped her purse on the front seat to look for something.

"They're gone, Mom."

"Who's gone, Charlie?"

"The Carters, Mom. All of them are gone. And so is all their furniture and even the dogs. They even took the barking dog. You'd think they'd just leave him for the neighbors to take care of, since we've gotten used to him howling."

"What?" Mom said.

I kind of looked at her. I'd just told her all about the disappearance of the Carters, and she hadn't even heard me. I guess it wasn't a good idea to bug Mom when she was on her way to work.

She smiled, then kissed me on the top of my head like I was a baby. (I wish she wouldn't.)

"You shouldn't tease that dog, Charlie."

"What?" I said.

"You shouldn't tease that dog of the Carters'."

Then she started the car and blew a kiss at me as she pulled out of the drive. She rolled down the window and called, "Pay attention to Sid. And try to eat something sensible. I don't think a hundred cookies a day is a well-balanced diet."

Well, paying attention to Sid was not something I wanted to think about, but I would try not to eat so many cookies. I was spending most of my days eating them.

A good cookie can be the best thing in the world.

That's when I went into the house to tell Sid about the Carters. Sid said we should be careful, 'cause if the mystery is what we all think it is (that a whole family just disappeared with aliens or something), we could *all* disappear. Just like the Carter family. But I caught him giggling as he left the kitchen. I might as well have been talking to one of my neighbor Mr. Pinkton's fish. Sid is never much help, but sometimes he can be such a pest that I feel like gluing a sign around his body that says

ANNOYING BROTHER FOR SALE.

I decided I'd go tell Lump and Billy all about

the Carters. They'd believe me, and maybe even help me find out what happened to them.

Lump's uncle let me into their kitchen.

"And what have we done to have the honor of your presence, Miss Charlie, on such a fine morning as this?"

Lump's uncle always talks like that. I just smile a lot and look confused. A lot. I did say yes to the muffins he offered me, though. I sat in their sunny kitchen waiting for Lump to come down and remembered what Mom said about a well-balanced diet. I ate only three blueberry muffins....

"What's up, Charlieroo?"

Lump was wearing a superhero T-shirt and still looked sleepy. I felt kind of bad because I know Lump likes to sleep late. Summer vacation to Lump is eating as much fruit as he can and sleeping as late as his aunt and uncle will let him.

He'd found me with muffin in my mouth, so it took me a while to tell him what I wanted to. He sat down in the sunny yellow kitchen beside me and started eating muffins, too.

"Lump."

"Yeah."

"The Carters are gone. I went to their house a while ago, and everyone and everything is gone. Dogs and furniture. *Everything* is gone."

"Wow!" Lump said.

I almost fell on the floor when Lump got excited. He hadn't put in his morning gum yet. So I know he said "Wow!" Sometimes you really can't understand Lump when he has a mouthful of gum.

Lump moved closer to my chair.

"What do you think happened to them, Charlie?"

"I don't know, but I think we should find out."

We said at the same time, "Let's go get Billy."

Well, I don't think Billy ever sleeps at all. I remember his mother once saying she thinks she's slept maybe a total of twelve hours since Billy has been able to walk. I told my dad that, and he laughed so hard I thought he was going to bust a gut. I don't know why that was so funny.

Anyway, Billy was up. That is, actually he was down—hanging upside down from a branch of the tree in his backyard.

The first thing he said when we found him was "Did you know the Carters have disappeared?"

You have to have mystery gear.

I have it and have been waiting to use it for about a year.

It includes a big orange flashlight, a magnifying glass, fingerprint powder, binoculars, a coil of rope, and a packet of cheese crackers in case I fall into a dungeon and can't be found for a few days. Lump and Billy supplied bottles of water and some crab apples from the disappeared Carters' tree.

I said, "Billy, you look in the side windows. Lump, you look in the front ones, and I'll go around to the back to look through the kitchen window."

It was still pretty early in the morning, but looking through the window of the Carters' empty house was kind of like walking through a scary house at midnight. The strange thing was there was not so much as one piece of paper left on the floor of the house.

How did a big family like the Carters just disappear and not even leave shoes or something behind? We weren't going to find out what happened to them by just looking in through the windows…so I climbed up the backyard trellis to the roof.

I loved being up high, even though I still didn't find out what happened to everybody. I did scare Lump and Billy real bad, though, when I howled down at them.

They ran around to the front of the house before I could tell them it was me. I got them good.

Boy, was that funny!

Lump and Billy even thought so. I found them lying on their backs underneath the Carters' crab apple tree, laughing, and I laughed with them.

"Good one, Charlie," Billy said.

"Yeah, I thought the ghosts or aliens who took the Carters were just about to jump down on us," said Lump.

Lump finally stood up, blew a bubble, and

said, "What next? I don't think an empty house is going to tell us what happened to the Carters."

He was right. All the evidence was gone.

"We'll have to start questioning everybody in the neighborhood today. I'm sure somebody has seen something."

Billy said, "What if they won't talk?"

Maybe the neighbors would think it wasn't our business to know anything. I said, "Well, we'll just have to trick them into talking. Or if they're anything like us, they are pretty nosy and want to talk."

So we walked around Magnolia Street looking for neighbors to question. When we caught somebody outside, we acted sort of friendly, then asked a million questions about the Carters. Billy wrote down everything.

Ms. Multree lives on the right side of the Carters. She said:

"Don't know where they went, but I got a

good night's sleep for the first time since they brought home Woof."

"Who's Woof?" I asked.

"That barking dog of theirs is Woof."

"I thought the dog's name was Peanut."

"It was Woof to me because that's the only thing that ever came out of his mouth."

Then Ms. Multree almost skipped away down the sidewalk. She didn't miss the Carters one bit!

Mr. Warren, who lives on the other side of the Carters, said, "Who?"

We really never see Mr. Warren out in the daytime. Back in the winter I thought he might be a vampire, but Mom says he worked nights. He was kind of pale, though, and a little confused about who the Carters were.

Billy said, "Well, he was no help."

The rest of the neighborhood was no help, either. It was almost like the Carters had never been there. It was almost like ten kids never tore through the neighborhood or emptied the ice cream truck before anybody else got Popsicles or beat everybody who challenged them in football.

I looked down the ravine with my binoculars to make sure the Carters weren't living there. Billy sprinkled fingerprint powder all over the neighborhood and lost the rope when running from Mrs. Perkins after accidentally sprinkling her just-washed car.

Lump fed the cheese crackers to the Perkinses' cats while he was using the magnifying glass on them to count their fleas.

We were exhausted from a day of being spies.

The sun was going down on Magnolia Street. We all sat in my front yard feeling tired and unworthy of spyhood.

I waved to Lump and Billy as they dragged themselves home.

A MYSTERY (WHERE'RE THE CARTERS?)

I went to sleep swatting a mosquito away and wondering what happened to the Carters.

Well, like I said at the beginning, this mystery didn't start off like the ones in books. No one saw them leave or knew they were leaving, but the Carters were gone. Dad said it was a real conundrum. When I looked confused, he said that was the same as a mystery.

Sometimes, though, a mystery isn't a mystery at all. Sometimes it's just that you don't have the information. And sometimes it helps if you leave your neighborhood with your friends to buy fish food and guppies for Mr. Pinkton.

Billy was holding the bag of guppies we had just bought at The Sea Hut. I love going to The Sea Hut. Me, Lump, and Billy stayed there for hours looking at the fish. We always feel better after leaving The Sea Hut.

You can get pretty sad when you're a failed spy. (And we were sad.)

But just as we were walking out of The Sea Hut, something went running by us. Peanut Carter! We knew it was him by his woof.

"C'mon!" I yelled.

The chase was on. We chased Peanut all over and under town. He was one fast little dog. Just a hint about how horrible it was for us to follow Peanut: Only dogs and a few other four-legged animals can crawl under barbecue grills.

I ripped my pants, Billy lost his hat, and Lump lost a shoe...but...we found the Carters!

I was pretty disappointed I wasn't a good enough spy to figure out what happened to the Carters, but we know now....

Nothing!

That's what Ben Carter said while he was

standing in their yard on Maple Grove Road squirting people who walked by while one of his sisters swung in the hammock and another one sold lemonade in front of their bigger house.

When I told Sid that the Carters had moved in the middle of the night 'cause that was the only time they could get a truck, he laughed.

"I knew it all the time," he said. "Ben came over for boxes a few days before they moved. Mystery, huh?" Sid laughed again.

Something very mysterious is happening on Magnolia Street.

All of my brother Sid's skateboards and in-line skates just up and disappeared. Nobody knows what happened to them. I told him it must be a mystery. I figure any good mystery can start in an attic. And that's exactly where they are.

Although when Sid's not home, me, Lump, and Billy roll all over Magnolia Street on his skateboards and skates.

We might come across a mystery on a dark road or have to chase a fast dog. Spies need wheels.

CHAPTER THREE

Magic

There's magic now, on Magnolia Street.

A couple of weeks ago the Magics bought the Carters' house, and nothing will ever be the same on our street again.

In the beginning the Magics' moving day looked a lot like the day my family moved to Magnolia Street last summer. People were yelling for kids to get out of the way of the movers. Boxes that sounded like they were filled with glass tumbled down the stairs.

Me and Lump and Billy watched from underneath the crab apple tree in the front yard of the Magics' house as the boxes and furniture moved out of the truck, up the porch stairs, and through the door.

The Magics have two teenage girls. They waved to us every now and then when they weren't carrying things into the house. They looked like they might be fun. We all smiled and waved back.

Their dad came out and waved at us, too. A few seconds later he looked at them and said something, then looked at us and waved his arm around the girls.

With a puff of smoke, the girls disappeared....

Wow!

Magic on Magnolia Street.

Billy jumped up.

"Where'd they go?"

I jumped up, too.

"They disappeared, right in front of us."

Lump jumped up and blew a bubble. He

didn't say anything, but the bubble grew huge, then exploded all over his face.

Billy asked, "Where do you think they went?"

"Gone," I said.

"Gone where?" Billy asked.

Lump pulled a crab apple off the tree and took a bite out of it. How he can chew gum and eat food at the same time, I have no idea.

"It's magic. They aren't really anywhere. They're in Magicland."

Me and Billy looked at him and smiled. Lump's eyes were shining like they had never shined before.

"I've always wanted to be a magician," he said.

"You'd make a good magician, Lump. I've seen you make a lot of things disappear. It was mostly food, but I was pretty amazed how it was there, then all of a sudden it wasn't."

Billy and Lump laughed and ate more crab apples. I ate the crab apples, too, but I was still hungry. I wasn't going to leave, though, until the two girls appeared again.

We waited.

Their dad carried more boxes into the house. It looked like it might take hours to unpack the moving truck. After a while he started helping the movers with furniture.

My stomach started to growl.

The crab apple cores started to pile up beside Lump and Billy, and bees started to buzz around the cores.

I figured my mom had probably been looking for me to eat dinner. It was time to give up waiting for the disappeared girls. I turned to leave.

"I have to go home now," I said.

As soon as Lump and Billy started complaining that the girls were bound to reappear any minute, the dad came out again. This time he had on a black cape. He nodded to us, then whirled his cape around.

And then one, two, three…the girls were there.

What a great trick! We clapped and stomped our feet. The girls and their father bowed, waved, then went inside the house.

I skipped home fast, yelling good-bye to Lump and Billy as I ran up our front steps and through the door.

Mom was just setting the table. Sid was complaining about not getting more allowance. Dad was stirring chili on the stove.

"I just saw two girls disappear into thin air," I said.

"Oh yeah?" Sid asked.

"Yeah, and then a while later their dad made them magically reappear."

Sid said, "Why didn't you ask if you could go with them?"

"Funny, Sid. I'd rather ask them to make you disappear, then forget how to get you back."

Dad laughed. "Maybe I should go talk to the man and find out how he does that trick."

Mom laughed, too, real hard. In a minute she and Dad were giggling so much that Mom had to stop putting out the napkins and Dad had to step away from the stove. Me and Sid, for once, agreed that the joke wasn't funny.

Dad wiped his eyes with his sleeve and finally stopped laughing. Mom giggled a little more and winked at him.

"Sounds like we have a family of magicians in the neighborhood."

We all sat down to eat. I love my dad's chili. He always uses our garden tomatoes.

I ate two bowls and I think Sid ate about a gallon.

I asked Mom, "Do you think I could learn magic?"

"Sure, Charlie. Magic is a matter of practice, practice, and more practice."

"I can practice," I said.

Everybody knows I can. I just started playing the trumpet. It took me a long time to pick out the instrument I wanted to play. Mrs. Walker, my music teacher, helped me make my decision. She was great and told me that if I practice a lot, I could be a great trumpet player.

That's all it took.

I've been practicing ever since summer vacation began.

I practice early in the morning before anyone gets up. I practice in the living room while everybody is there. I want them to hear how good I'm getting. Mostly, though, I practice alone in the garden.

Mom says she thinks the plants will enjoy the music so much more than the walls in the house will. She says music will help them grow. She even set out a comfortable chair for me to sit in. She seems real happy about me sharing my music with the vegetable garden. She even brings my snacks outdoors.

So everybody knows I can practice.

I thought about magic all through dinner and way past the time I was supposed to be in bed sleeping.

I looked out the window toward the magician's house, imagining the wonderful kinds of magic that were going on there.

Maybe they were making elephants and many different kinds of wild animals appear and disappear. You never know what kind of magic is out there.

Lump was in our front yard early the next morning. He had one of his aunt's tablecloths slung around his shoulders like a cape.

"What do you think?" he said.

"You look good," I said.

"I'm ready for magic," he said.

So we walked to the old Carter house and camped out on the front lawn underneath the crab apple tree again.

What would happen next?

Well, something happened sooner than we thought. One of the Magic girls walked out of the house and waved us over. She was wearing a ballet tutu and a baseball cap.

"Hi, I'm Chris. Were you two here yesterday?"

"That was us," I said. "I'm Charlie, and the guy in the cape is Lump."

"Hi," Lump said.

"Hi," Chris giggled. "I like your cape."

"That was pretty cool the way you and your sister went away in a cloud of smoke," Lump said.

"Do you guys want to come in?" Chris asked.

Lump almost swallowed his gum. I think he

had a hard time not running up to the house. I was excited about going into the Magic house, too. Maybe I'd see some wild animals left over from a few magic tricks.

We walked into the front hall and saw a huge banner that read

THE GREAT VICTORIO

"That's my dad. He's been The Great Victorio ever since I've known him. He's been doing magic all his life, he says."

Past the Great Victorio sign to the left was a room with nothing but trunks and boxes that looked like they were used in magic acts. There was even a long wood box that was cut in half.

Chris said, "My dad can put someone in there and saw them in two."

"Wow," Lump said.

He went over to the box and looked under and around it. He knocked on the sides and crawled alongside it. Then he started looking at everything else in the room. I did, too.

I saw magic wands and hats, and empty boxes that Chris said would not be so empty during the tricks. There were stuffed animals and masks. There was an upright box that looked like a closet with a curtain across it (probably for making people disappear).

We didn't want to leave the magic room. Even Chris was excited, and she lives with magic all the time.

"Want to see a trick?" she asked.

"Oh yeah!" Lump and I yelled at the same time.

"This is the first trick my dad taught me."

Lump and I sat down on the crowded floor and watched. I thought I could actually hear Lump's heart beating. What could Chris do?

What would appear or disappear?

Would there be wild animals? Fireworks?

Chris bowed.

"Thank you all for coming to the show. Now you will witness the most incredible feat of conjuring the world has ever seen."

Lump whispered, "What's conjuring?"

"Magic," I whispered back.

Chris took off her baseball cap and put on a top hat. She did some turns and clapped her hands. She walked slowly over to the box with the curtain across it.

"As you both can see, this closet is empty." She opened the curtains, then turned the box around and tapped hard at the back.

"Ma'am," she said, meaning me, "would you like to make certain this box is empty?"

"Sure," I said.

I walked over to the closet. I checked for trapdoors or anything like that.

"Yes, it's empty." There was no way anybody could get past us in the room.

I sat back down beside Lump, who was so excited that he hadn't blown a bubble since we'd come into the house. It was a shame Billy was missing this. We should have gone by his house to get him. Suddenly I felt pretty bad about his not being there.

I knew how excited he'd been the night before.

Chris circled the closet, then turned it around toward us. She bent to pick up a wand beside it and bowed again and pointed the wand at the closet.

"ABRACADABRA, ABRACABOO!"

There was a puff of blue smoke, then a sneeze.

Someone was in the closet now!

"It's somebody with hay fever," Lump whispered.

Chris walked over and threw the curtain back. Out stepped a person in a mask and a hat, and covered in a big cape.

Me and Lump clapped and yelled for a long time.

Chris and the masked person bowed to us and stepped back into the closet. Suddenly there was another puff of blue smoke, a big one. Then we heard Chris's voice.

"Please open the curtain."

We did, and there was no one there. Then another puff, and there were Chris and the masked person.

They both bowed again.

It was a fantastic trick!

Chris said, "Please come again to our show."

"That was great," Lump said as we walked down the sidewalk toward my house.

"Yeah, it was. Only, I'm sorry Billy missed it."

"Me too," he said.

Lump and I walked quietly down Magnolia Street, dreaming of magic.

Billy was waiting for us when we got back to my house.

"You missed it, Billy," I said.

"Wow, did you miss it," Lump said. "We went to the magic house, and Chris, one of the girls from yesterday, did a great disappearing act for us."

Billy looked upset.

"Why didn't you guys come and get me? I would have loved to see the magic up close."

Then we really felt bad. We didn't know how we would make it up to Billy. That is, we felt really bad until Billy started to sneeze.

Lump looked at me. Then I looked at Billy.

Billy laughed and took off running.

We chased him, but all of a sudden he seemed to just disappear behind a hedge.

He'd beaten us to the magic on Magnolia Street.

CHAPTER FOUR

A Friend

Magnolia Street has been looking different these days. Even though Lump and Billy went to camp, I've been having fun. I guess sometimes people have to go away for you to know that you can be okay without them.

That's not to say that I don't miss my friends.

When I found all those baby raccoons living in my mom's garden shed, I really wanted to see what Lump and Billy would say about them. With the black around their eyes, they looked like little bandits. I've named all of them, and I'm hoping that their mom will come back, or

I'm going to have to get them help. They sure can eat a lot, though.

Also, I've been taking long walks all over the neighborhood. Sometimes when you're with your friends, you don't notice or think about certain things.

Like, did the lady who lives eight houses away always have that metal elephant in her front yard? Or, just how many cats *did* the Perkinses have this summer? And, if I hung around Mr. Church's front porch long enough, would he give me a ride in his Model T?

I love living on Magnolia Street, even when Lump and Billy aren't around. So I was pretty happy just feeding the raccoons and visiting Miss Marcia, my neighbor who's a sculptor, when *she* appeared.

It had been raining for days and days without the sun peeking outside the clouds even one time; and my brother, Sid, was being even more obnoxious than he usually was, and that's being a real big pest.

So maybe I was missing Lump and Billy a little. I'd think of them when I was running around eating ice cream and dodging in and out of Miss Marcia's sprinklers when she wasn't looking.

I never thought they'd leave Magnolia Street at the same time to go away to camp (only separately, because Billy's mom and Lump's aunt and uncle said they liked the camp counselors too much to send Lump and Billy together). Billy said he didn't get it, and Lump snickered and put more gum in his mouth.

I always laugh when I think of the way Lump can barely talk with that big wad of gum but can blow bubbles as big as his head. And how Billy is always hiding my shoes and calling me the Barefoot Sneaker 'cause I can go anywhere and get into anything without my shoes and never make a sound.

Once I even found my shoes in the refrigerator. Mom didn't think that was too funny and told us that if we didn't have anything better to do, we could go pull up all the weeds in the garden.

I thought about Lump and Billy as I sailed on through the time they were gone. I was having fun on my own on Magnolia Street. So it was a surprise when the hat girl appeared. Maybe there was going to be *more* fun on Magnolia Street.

You can always smell peanuts on Magnolia Street. It's a wonderful smell. Sometimes I just sit at my bedroom window and sniff....

But last night, just before the sun went down, when I raised my window to really smell the peanuts from the peanut butter factory, I saw something run through our backyard. A huge moving hat.

What was a huge straw hat doing rushing through our backyard?

People shouldn't be running around back-yards; at least people who aren't Lump or Billy or me shouldn't be running around backyards. They should be inside pretending they're taking a bath (while really just running the water and reading a comic book or eating the last of the cookies they took out of their brother's room). If you ask me, there aren't enough hours in the day to waste one on a bath.

So I called to the hat, "Hey, hat, what are you doing down there?"

The hat didn't answer.

I thought it might be a good idea to climb down the vines that run up to my window. Mom would never see me. I could probably catch the hat.

Unfortunately, just then Sid opened the door and squirted me with his water pistol. He ran out of the room so fast I couldn't throw something at him. I'd have to get him back later.

But as I was thinking some more about the hat, Sid sneaked in and hit me with a water balloon. I had to scream like he'd broken my arm to make sure Mom and Dad would come. When they got to me, Sid was gone, and when I tried to tell them what happened, they just shook their heads and talked about how they really should have sent us to camp.

When I finally got into dry pajamas, the moon was shining through my window. The hat was gone.

I dreamed of water balloons and hats all night long.

A FRIEND

* * *

The next morning Mom let me eat breakfast on the porch. I love eating outside. Food always tastes so much better, I think.

I was sitting on the porch swing munching on apples and enjoying the smell of the honeysuckle vines. Just as I was about to finish an apple off, core and all, the hat came back— going down the sidewalk.

I crawled off the porch swing and looked between the honeysuckle vines.

A girl about my size with lots of braids smiled up at me. She was pushing a wheelbarrow.

Well, all I have to say is that Sid didn't string up enough rope as a trellis for the honeysuckle, because it's obvious now that it isn't the best thing to hide behind when spying on someone. My face must have stuck out, 'cause the hat girl with the wheelbarrow waved to me. I smiled back at her and then remembered that my face was poking out of the honeysuckle. I must have looked pretty funny with honey-suckle hair.

There were all kinds of flowers and a shovel in the wheelbarrow. The hat girl stopped for only a few seconds, then kept on pushing the wheelbarrow down the sidewalk.

She looked at the flowers and trees in people's front yards as she walked.

Sometimes she even stopped and smelled flowers and touched bushes and trees. She smiled a lot and looked like she was having so much fun.

Mom came out on the porch and pulled me out of the honeysuckle.

"She's something, huh?"

"Who?" I said. I didn't want Mom to think I was spying.

"The girl with the wheelbarrow that you were watching."

Mom ate one of the apples on my plate and started the porch swing swaying.

I said, "So what do you think she does with the stuff in the wheelbarrow?"

Mom laughed. "What do *you* think?"

Suddenly Sid was out on the porch putting in his two cents.

"I think she eats all those flowers. She probably thought you were a plant with your head sticking out of those vines. She probably had never seen such a goofy-looking vine before and was going to come over and pull you up."

Just as I was about to pinch Sid, Mom coughed. Real loud and kind of fake, which usually means she's about to give that enough-is-enough look to me and Sid.

I couldn't wait to meet the hat girl, but I suddenly remembered that I owed Sid a little surprise. So I just smiled at him and went into the house.

I'd have the surprise for him later.

Early the next morning I found a pot of flowers on our front porch with a note beside it that said

THERE ARE SOME FLOWERS THAT

BLOOM ONLY IN THE MOONSHINE.

They were from the hat girl. I decided to plant them by the honeysuckle vines. It was the first thing I had ever planted. I usually run when Mom starts putting in the garden. I guess the planting part is never as good as the eating part to me. I was really proud of how that moon flower looked. And just when I was feeling so proud I was about to float up into the sky, the hat girl appeared.

She was still wearing her hat but didn't have the wheelbarrow. She stood on the front walk watching me.

"Thanks for the moon flower."

"You're welcome. Ashley."

"No, my name is Charlie," I said.

The hat girl almost fell over laughing, holding her stomach. Then I started laughing. Soon we were both on the ground laughing. Sid went by on his bike and just shook his head.

"My name is Ashley, but you can call me Ashe."

"Like I said, I'm Charlie."

Ashe and I sat there and talked for a long time. She told me everything about herself, and I told her everything about myself.

Ashe loves chocolate and can eat it anytime, day or night. She's spending the summer with her grandmother (who gardens, too) around the corner on Pine Street. She lives in Chicago but really loves it here on Magnolia Street.

She loves music. I love music.

Ashe loves animals, and so do I.

"But most of all, Charlie, I love to garden and save plants."

Me and Ashe spent the rest of the day walking around the neighborhood.

She'd point out different kinds of flowers and tell me what they were called in Latin. I'd point out everybody in the neighborhood and tell her who liked kids and who made the best cookies and muffins.

Then I took her on a swing through the trees.

You can tell a lot about someone who can swing from limb to limb without falling or screaming that their arms are falling off.

Ashley is okay.

She likes climbing trees and swinging from them almost more than me.

Ashley asked, when we finally sat down in my front yard, "Who's the lady with all the statues everywhere? She seems real funny. Did you see the upside-down penguin in her front yard? I love her flowers. She puts them in silly planters. There're even sunflowers in a bathtub. I think I'll like her."

"That's Miss Marcia. She's an artist and can bake the best muffins in the world. She's great. I'll take you to meet her."

And I did....

Ashley—I mean Ashe—wandered all over Miss Marcia's studio and rubbed the smooth marble and stone.

"It's great here. I think I could live in your studio forever—if you had more flowers, and vines growing up the statues."

Miss Marcia looked at Ashe for a long time, then said, "Well, why don't you help me out with that? I have a huge backyard full of art."

Ashley looked at the sculpture, then me, and smiled the biggest smile I'd ever seen.

The next few days all we did was collect dirt in wheelbarrows and flowers from different people. Sometimes I'd push Ashe in the wheelbarrow, and sometimes she'd push me. We were having a good time. I found out I really love dirt.

This is what Ashe said about plants that she got from people: "Pass-along plants are the best you can have. You can get plants that are a hundred years old. My dad has a rose bush that came from a garden that was started about ninety years ago. Just think of all the things these roses have heard and seen, Charlie."

I laughed thinking about a rose bush with ears and eyes, but I understood what she meant. All of a sudden the planting seemed more exciting to me, and I helped Ashe anytime she needed me. She said she was planting a pass-along garden for Miss Marcia's sculpture that might last a thousand years.

Wow!

When Ashe and I weren't planting, we were swinging from trees or eating peanut butter (my favorite). I told Ashe about Lump and Billy, and she told me about her friend Lily, who can play the piano with her toes.

Even though Ashe doesn't live on Magnolia Street, I feel like she belongs here.

We worked all week getting ready for the garden unveiling.

Me and Ashe made invitations for the party and painted them for what seemed like days. Mom helped by feeding us and not complaining that we were getting paint everywhere. We delivered the invitations on a hot, mosquito-filled evening to everybody I knew in the neighborhood.

We got some of the neighbors to donate snacks for the party. Of course Miss Marcia would bake muffins, and Billy's mom said she would make strawberry iced tea. Mr. Pinkton made peach pies that smelled so good I wondered if I could wait until the garden unveiling to eat it.

The only way this whole past week could have been better was if Billy and Lump had been here....

They would have loved the whole party idea.

The morning of the garden unveiling was cool and rainy, and Ashe said she hoped it wouldn't keep too many people away. We couldn't wait for the whole neighborhood to see the garden. Even Miss Marcia hadn't looked in her back-yard. She'd promised she wouldn't look.

About ten people with umbrellas showed up to see the garden. They squished down to Miss Marcia's backyard. I really couldn't see any-body's face for the rain hoods and scarves. Ashe and I stood beside each other.

And the garden...

Beautiful!

Vines climbed up sculptures of animals wearing hats. Flowers sat in birdbaths and were planted in marble pigs' ears. And best of all were the moon flowers winding around a statue of a spaceman.

Everybody clapped and walked around the beautiful, wet garden.

Ashe kept on smiling.

*   *   *

Sid didn't go to the garden party. Really, it was probably a good thing he didn't. I had gotten a great idea during the week while I was pushing dirt from here to there.

I wasn't at home when Sid started to yell.

I wasn't even going to be at home that night because I was having a sleep-over at Ashe's grandmother's house.

I was even thinking about moving out of our house and camping out in the woods for a few weeks.

When I did go home, though, Mom and Dad gave me what they call a good talking-to.

How would I feel, they asked, if I came home and found all my dresser drawers filled with dirt and planted with vines?

I didn't even mind having to sit on the porch for a week with Sid growling at me.

Funny how just a week ago I never thought I'd like gardening.

CHAPTER FIVE

Billy's Letter from Camp

Dear Charlie,

Well, I'm here, and I can't even believe I got here in one piece.

You know how in the beginning I didn't think camp was such a good idea? I did about everything I could to get the idea out of my mom's head.

I mean *everything*....

I hid the brochure that had come in the mail about Camp FunWa.

I cut out the newspaper article that talked about Camp FunWa so Mom wouldn't see it.

I disconnected the phone when my mom

was talking to my grandma about sending me to camp. (That time I got in real trouble, and that was the day Mom decided to send me.)

Thanks for hiding me in your mom's garden shed the night before I left. (I don't think the groundhog liked me being there too much. I figure he thought he'd lost his hiding place.) And anyway, he about scared me to death. If he had, I wouldn't have had to come to Camp FunWa. What's with that name, anyhow? And how does my mom know how to find me anywhere I hide?

Well, like I said, we barely got here.

My mom jumps to conclusions—that's why she thought I'd gotten lost at the gas station.

But if you talk to her, she'll tell you a different story. I won't tell you not to believe her, but just don't take her too serious, 'cause she's always getting upset about stuff that isn't that important.

I wasn't *hiding* when she found me in the bushes behind the gas station between some old cars. See, there was this strange thing I saw when I was coming out of the gas station bathroom. I was pretty lucky to even get out of the bathroom, 'cause the lock broke when I was in there and I had to climb through the vent in the bottom of the door.

Nobody heard me yelling. I guess that's because I couldn't get the sink turned off. Charlie, I thought I was gonna drown in the Speedy Gas bathroom.

Water was everywhere.

I got blamed for that, too.

Anyway, I followed what I thought was an alien to the back of the gas station. It turned out to be a cat. He was all spotted and kind of nice to share his hiding place with me. Anyway, I was petting him and lost track of time. It's true!

Mom and the gas station man didn't believe me. Neither did the police. I guess I had been gone for an hour or so.

Anyway, here I am. At Camp FunWa.

Charlie, there's a huge lake that surrounds the camp. It's almost like we're on an island. Mom said something about liking the idea that we almost can't get out of camp without taking a boat. There is a way out without a boat. You just have to find it, but they keep us so busy that who has time to find the way out of Camp Fun*Not*? That's what most of the campers call it.

I'm glad you went with me to buy all the good junk food to bring here (even if the counselors found my hiding place in the lining of my suitcase and took it away from me). The green bean casserole we had last night was real bad. I mean, on a good day I love green beans, but I don't think those green beans ever had a good day.

One of the older kids said the only food they ever serve here is green beans, cheese, and mystery meat.

I do like all the guys in my cabin, though. So far, we all get along. I think I even made a new friend. His name is Sam, and he can blow even bigger bubbles than Lump can. Don't tell Lump, though.

I think I'm going to be okay here because of Sam. That is, if we don't get separated from each other. One of the counselors keeps saying he doesn't think we're very good influences on each other.

Well, I'm used to people saying that about me and most of my friends. Me, you, and Lump wouldn't be friends at all if we listened to that kind of talk. Sam is a lot of fun, and it's not just that he blows milk through his nose when he starts laughing or that he got his head stuck in the fence that leads to the herb garden that us campers planted the second day after we got here.

We're friends because he laughs with me at all the stuff that goes wrong.

Sometimes it's not so good that he laughs real loud, though. He probably could have laughed quieter when we got locked in the food pantry in the camp kitchen. We were just looking for a few cookies. I knew they had them in there, 'cause we saw a few of the counselors munching on them when we were supposed to be resting.

Can you believe it—they were peanut butter!

Charlie, you know how I love peanut butter cookies. There just wasn't any way I could pass them up. I hadn't seen a cookie in a couple of days. We got fruit for lunch. I think it was supposed to be good for us, so I thought I needed cookies. Sam thought we needed cookies, too.

So, after everybody had gone to their cabins to rest and the counselors were down by the lake relaxing, we thought we had a clear path to the kitchen. Well, we got into the kitchen okay.

Then we got to the pantry okay. The key was hanging right by the door. (Why?) We put it back before we went in.

We got the pantry open okay. Then we saw all the food. Boy, was there a lot of food! We were minutes from all kinds of cookies, dried fruit, and boxes of chocolate when we heard laughing. Sam and I hid behind a big box of canned peaches. We closed our eyes, hoping we wouldn't get caught, so that's why we didn't know until it was too late that the doors had been closed and the pantry light had been turned off.

I think we could have broken out of there. We sure did try. I don't know why those locks are so strong. Do you think they're trying to

keep kids out of the pantry?! They should feed us better at camp.

Anyway, by the time we had finished a few bags of cookies, me and Sam were so full and so sick of them that I didn't care if I never saw another cookie again my whole life. I think Sam felt the same as I did.

We would have gotten away with it if Sam hadn't start laughing in his sleep.

Later he said he was dreaming about everybody wandering around the camp with pants on their heads. I couldn't wake him up and that's how they found us. Surrounded by empty cookie boxes, and Sam laughing in his sleep.

We're sticking to our stories that everything was all right with us, too. I guess everybody had been looking for us a few hours, and they had been so upset that they'd called our parents. Mr. Rufus, the camp director, told us our parents had come up with our punishments. It's always good to know my mom is thinking about me. Sam said he wished his parents wouldn't think about him as much as they do.

Peeling potatoes for the whole camp's meals isn't so bad. I make a game of it.

Sam says washing dishes isn't that bad, either.

And mystery meat isn't looking all that bad anymore at old Camp FunWa.

It's been only four days, Charlie. How is everything on Magnolia Street?

Lots of wishes that you don't get kisses!

Your friend,
Billy

CHAPTER SIX

A Letter from Lump

Dear Charlie,

How have you been doing way on the other side of the state? Is Magnolia Street still sitting there waiting for me to come back to it? I (Oops—I got to stop writing for a minute to get all this gum off my shirt.)

Well, Charlie, it's about forty-five minutes later. I was in a little trouble with the gum. Who knew it was so sticky?...I kind of got some in this girl's hair when she tried to get it off my shirt. (It's a good thing the girls will be on the other side of the lake.) Then a counselor tried to help, and it ended up all on his glasses.

I'm not supposed to be chewing it. I'll tell you why later.

(I should probably start chewing a different kind that doesn't stick so much.)

Camp Margaret is great. I really didn't think I would be very happy here, but I'm surprised at how much fun everything is.

When my aunt and uncle decided—along with Billy's mom—that it wouldn't be a good idea for us to go to camp together, I thought it might be one of the worst summers in the world. I mean, what would I do without Billy and you! But it's working out.

Camp Margaret is an art camp.

I have never painted on so many things in my life—and you don't get yelled at for doing it.

Yesterday we got to paint each other. It was crazy.

First everybody had to wear white T-shirts

and shorts. Then the counselors sprayed us with water and handed each of us a palette full of all different colors of paint and a brush. The painting party was on....

In the end everyone was just smearing paint on each other and wearing their palettes as hats. I looked like a huge tie-dyed walking thing. For some reason this boy named Pip was covered only in yellow paint. We all started calling him Banana Boy.

The counselors thought we looked great and took pictures. The fun didn't last long, though. The camp owner showed up with a tour of parents. We found out later we were only supposed to be painting each other's T-shirts.

The counselors had to go to a meeting afterward. But they were laughing when they came out, and the camp owner just shook his head a lot and took off in his car real fast.

I love camp.

Charlie...we have a real live (dead, really) ghost at Camp Margaret. And I saw him! That's kind of why I'm not supposed to be chewing gum.

It all started on the bus trip out here. Our parents had to drop us off at the huge mall over by Lake Blackhorse. The camp bus would pick us up and take us the two hours to camp. It was fun on the bus—meeting everybody and laughing. There were only a couple of kids who had been to Camp Margaret before. But they told the same story....

It was a story about a kid whose parents forgot to pick him up at camp. He stayed there for a few days waiting for them—but finally got tired and went to live in the woods. He liked it so much he decided he would never go back to the suburbs. He lived off berries and wild animals. He grew older in the woods and made a house in a cave.

His parents would come at the beginning of each summer and try to lure him out of the woods with peanut butter sandwiches (his favorite), but it never worked. He was tricky and would always manage to get the sandwiches but not get captured. His parents finally gave up, deciding he would be happier in the woods.

Well, the kid grew up till one day the counselors at the camp figured he was about one hundred years old. Even though there had been a lot of sightings of him through the years—running, or swinging from tree to tree—there came a time when no one saw him for a whole summer. Everybody figured the old camper had finally passed on.

The next summer came and went, then a few more summers after that. But one night during a campfire sing-along, the Ghost of Camp Margaret was seen for the very first time....

These two kids who were sneaking out of the sing-along to pour honey in the counselors' hiking boots saw him walking by the entrance gate, a little old stooped-over man in a Camp Margaret T-shirt and a backpack. They say he was waiting for his parents to come and take him home from camp....

Now, that pretty much scared me while these kids were talking about it on the bus. I didn't want anybody to know it scared me, so I just laughed with everybody else, even though some of the kids' eyes got as big as mine while the story was being told. So three days later...

It's a shame sometimes that I have to chew so much gum all the time. (My aunt has been trying to break me of my bubble-blowing habit for a while. I think it's impossible.) Anyway, I started keeping emergency gum hidden in the knothole of this huge maple tree by the kitchen. I'd guess it was about two in the morning when I was woken out of a sound sleep by the need to blow a bubble.

I was kind of sleepy as I sneaked out of the cabin, hopping over Mickey Howard's Bigfoot trap (he thinks Bigfoot lives in the woods). I was really needing to blow a big bubble and really didn't pay attention to much else except finding the tree in the dark when all of a sudden there *he* was, the ghost camper, with a backpack on, by the kitchen, almost glowing in the dark.

Charlie, I couldn't even yell for help I was so scared.

The ghost of Camp Margaret was right in front of me!

Okay, okay, Charlie, it's not like that time I thought I saw the Loch Ness monster in Krieger's Pond. And it's not like that time I saw the pterodactyl flying over the bridge that runs past Magnolia Street.

This was different.

I fell to my knees and crawled real fast back to my cabin. Boy, is there a lot of stuff on the ground you don't notice when you're walking straight up, on your feet. I was really moving, Charlie. I knew nobody was going to believe me about the ghost. I had to wake up somebody. Unfortunately, I woke up *everybody*. Absolutely everybody in the camp.

Just as I was about to pull open the cabin door and wake up Mickey, his Bigfoot trap caught me.

The next thing that happened was a huge blanket was being tossed on me, and about the whole cabin was screaming that they had caught Bigfoot....

I kept screaming that I wasn't Bigfoot and that I was about to smother underneath the blanket.

Mickey kept screaming, "Listen to Bigfoot! He can talk!"

By that time the whole camp was awake, and all I could think of was how they'd scared the Camp Margaret ghost out of its skin and no one would believe I'd seen it.

Well, I'm not allowed to chew gum until the end of camp now. The camp director, Mr. Watson, lectured Mickey and me all about imagination and thought maybe painting the fence alongside the stables might help us burn off some energy.

You know, I get tired of people thinking I need to burn off energy. I think I'd like to keep my energy for a day when I might need it full strength. (I needed it when the whole cabin was sitting on me thinking I was Bigfoot.)

It's been a hard last few days. I don't like painting fences so much. Painting people is a whole lot better.

And the Camp Margaret ghost...

I know he's still out there—waiting to go home.

I STILL LOVE CAMP, CHARLIE!

BUT I HATE FENCES!

Your friend,
Lump

CHAPTER SEVEN

When Mules Flew on Magnolia Street

Dear Lump and Billy,

(Hope you two don't mind me sending you both the same letter.) I hope you guys got my last letter. I've missed you and can't wait to see you two next week. It hasn't been the same here since Camp FunWa and Camp Margaret grabbed both of you away from Magnolia Street.

I've met a real fun person from Chicago named Ashley while you two have been away at camp. I know we'll all have fun together when you guys meet her. She likes to plant things, and I'm starting to not mind gardening so much. I even pick vegetables instead of giving Sid half my allowance to do it for me.

I'm sorry you guys have been having a few problems at camp, but I know you're having fun anyway. How could you not?

Not much has been happening in the last couple of days. Ashley is visiting relatives in the country. Everybody has been so busy that mostly I just sit reading underneath the willow trees and drink lemonade all day long.

My dad says I have what he calls a good life.

But guess what?

I've been hanging out with Sid.

Yeah, my brother, Sid. The one who teases me and plays tricks on me and once even filled my room with so many frogs it took me days to find all of them.

I shouldn't say not much has been happening. I really meant to say not much is happening *now*. There have been a few things going on....

You see, mules have been flying over Magnolia Street.

No, really.

Really!

I didn't know I'd ever see such a thing. My brother, Sid, was the reason it all happened.

Do you guys ever wake up right as the sun is rising? Do you ever hear the man with the cart rolling down Magnolia Street singing this song?

> *Strawberries,*
> *Raspberries,*
> *Blueberries,*
> *Fresh in the crates.*
> *Sweet, sweet melons,*
> *Sweet, sweet grapes.*

Well, even if you never woke up to hear him, you probably ate some of the fruit off his cart, 'cause everybody in the neighborhood buys fruit from Mr. Janks.

I wake up just to listen to him calling through the streets. It wouldn't be summer without him.

Well, what I didn't know about Mr. Janks is that the mule pulling his cart is called Sweet Shirley and he's had her for twenty years. I finally got to meet her a few days ago.

She's great. She brays and swishes her tail when she sees me.

Sid is the one who introduced us all to each other. Sid says he and Mr. Janks have been friends for a long time. They know each other from our old neighborhood. Sid says Mr. Janks used to give him grapes when he'd see Sid on his paper route.

Who knew Sid was that likable?

I didn't, but it seems Mr. Janks and Sweet Shirley think so.

So—I guess you want to know how Sweet

Shirley ended up flying over Magnolia Street.

In the beginning it's a real sad story.

You see, one morning Mr. Janks didn't sing on Magnolia Street.

Then he wasn't there the next day, either.

Or the next…

At first I didn't notice, 'cause I just didn't wake up early. You see, the only reason I ever knew about Mr. Janks was that he woke me up singing. So without him and Sweet Shirley going down the street singing their song, I just slept in.

Well, Sid noticed. By the second day he was kind of worried.

Mom said, "Mr. Janks probably took a vacation."

"He never has before," Sid said.

"Mr. Janks is getting older now, though," Dad said, flipping pancakes. "He probably needs to take a rest."

Sid still looked worried. And worst of all, he didn't eat his breakfast. If you know Sid, you'll know that means he was *really* worried. There've been only a couple of times in his whole life that he didn't eat a meal.

He eats a lot even when he's sick.

He looked so sad that I got worried. (And I try never to worry about Sid, 'cause just about the time you have nice feelings about him, he does something mean or makes fun of you.)

Anyway, we were both worried.

Sid decided he'd go to Mr. Janks's house if he didn't show up the next day.

The next morning Sid and I waited in our pajamas, barefoot in the front yard, for Mr. Janks.

Sid said, "You don't have to wait with me."

"I want to. I miss Mr. Janks, too."

The sun was getting hot when we finally gave up. I held Sid's hand as we walked up the steps to go back into the house. He didn't even pull his hand away. He just looked out the window the whole day long.

I stayed close to the house that day. Sid wouldn't eat or skateboard or hang out with his friends. We played checkers all day long.

He didn't even come to the dinner table that night.

I told my mom and dad about Mr. Janks. It had been three days since he last showed up. Dad said, "If he doesn't come tomorrow, we'll go to his house."

"Thanks, Dad," Sid said. He'd been standing in the doorway of the kitchen.

Sid smiled and looked happier than he had in days, but we all were worried.

Mr. Janks lives in a little vine-covered house past the old mill, a couple of miles from

Magnolia Street. Me and Sid rode our bikes to his house. Dad said he'd drive to Mr. Janks's house when he was done mowing the lawn, in about twenty minutes.

Sid said, "I've been here before. Mr. Janks taught me to play chess last summer. He also let me feed Sweet Shirley. She loves apples."

We wouldn't do anything until Dad got there, so we sat in Mr. Janks's honeysuckle-filled front yard and watched the butterflies cover everything, even us.

Sweet Shirley started braying in the back, though, so we had to go see about her.

We found her in the little barn behind Mr. Janks's house. When she saw us, she got excited and started running back and forth in her stall. She ran up to us and nibbled at our hands.

We petted Sweet Shirley for a while, and she calmed down.

But, Lump and Billy, I have to tell you, my

dad almost scared us to death when he came into the barn.

"Hi, kids," he said. He came over and petted Sweet Shirley. "Mr. Janks is pretty sick. He's going to have to go to the hospital."

Sid looked so scared. "Will he be okay?" he asked.

Dad petted Sweet Shirley some more and said, "I hope so."

The ambulance came for Mr. Janks. He looked very sick when they took him away, but he asked me and Sid to take care of Sweet Shirley. We told him we would.

So that's what we did.

We made sure she went for walks and got all the apples she wanted. I loved taking care of her. Most important, though, was that me and Sid shared taking care of Sweet Shirley. We never fought, or even made fun of each other.

Sid visited Sweet Shirley in the morning,

and I took care of her in the afternoon. We both were with her in the evening. She liked the company, but we could tell she missed Mr. Janks.

She would suddenly look past us when she heard a noise. Then she would sort of gallop— thinking it was Mr. Janks. It was sad. She missed Mr. Janks so bad. And if she was missing him, he was probably missing her, too.

Poor Mr. Janks and Sweet Shirley.

Well, guys, we couldn't visit Mr. Janks in the hospital because me and Sid caught colds walking Sweet Shirley in the rain. Mom didn't think it would be good for Mr. Janks to catch a cold. But Mr. Janks sent us a note. It said:

Thank you, Sid and Charlie.
You are doing a kind thing taking

care of Sweet Shirley. You are also helping me get well. Hello to Sweet Shirley. Tell her I miss her.

Mr. Janks

We had to do something about Mr. Janks and Shirley. Dad said it would be a while before Mr. Janks got out of the hospital.

Sid and I thought about what we could do. We thought for a long time.

We couldn't take Shirley to the hospital, and Mr. Janks couldn't even get up to see her at the window if we did.

Sid said we should sleep on it.

That worked! 'Cause the next morning I had an idea for how Mr. Janks could see Sweet Shirley.

* * *

Remember when we made piñatas?

It took me and Sid a long time to make a Sweet Shirley piñata.

We had to go all over town to find a balloon big enough for Sweet Shirley's body. And we must have used all the newspaper in the neighborhood to glue onto the balloons. Everyone was helpful and gave us paints and anything we asked for.

Even Mr. Warren (the vampire) gave us rope that we needed. He said he likes Mr. Janks. He buys strawberries from him all the time.

Mom and Dad let us stay up late until the piñata was done. The next morning, there was Sweet Shirley life-size in our front yard on Magnolia Street.

Everybody in the neighborhood came out to see her.

Miss Marcia tied Sweet Shirley to the top of

her pickup. And, boy, was it a sight—a mule flying down Magnolia Street.

Sweet Shirley was beautiful, and she had *wings*. She'd need them if she was going to be hoisted down from the hospital roof so Mr. Janks could see her.

And that's what Dad and a couple of orderlies did.

We stood outside Mr. Janks's room as Sweet Shirley flew down from the roof and hung in front of his window for a while. Mr. Janks laughed and laughed. He'd missed her so much, and you know, it sounds silly, but that evening for the first time since Mr. Janks had gone into the hospital, the real Sweet Shirley seemed happy, too.

So, guys, that's what's been happening on Magnolia Street. Something else happened, too, that's kind of strange. Yesterday Sid asked me if I wanted to ride bikes with him up to the

park. And afterward—you won't believe this—
he broke his candy bar in half and shared it with
me....

You never know what's going to come down
Magnolia Street.

It's not camp, but it's okay.

Love,

Charlie

Angela Johnson is the author of one other book about Charlie—*Maniac Monkeys on Magnolia Street*—which is about her first summer on Magnolia Street. In addition, Ms. Johnson has written several other books for young readers, including *Songs of Faith; Gone from Home; Toning the Sweep*, for which she received the Coretta Scott King Award; and *Do Like Kyla*, illustrated by James Ransome. Born in Tuskegee, Alabama, she moved with her family to Ohio at a young age. Although she has lived there ever since, she enjoys traveling—when she isn't busy writing or wrangling gigantic goldfish.